HENSEL AND GRETEL NINJA CHICKS

To my favorite
Ninja neighbors,
Nika and Alik
— CRS

To David,
my own stealthy ninja
— RG

For Jodi
— DS

ISBN 978-1-338-20386-8

Text copyright © 2016 by Corey Rosen Schwartz and Rebecca J. Gomez.
Illustrations copyright © 2016 by Dan Santat. All rights reserved. Published by Scholastic Inc.,
557 Broadway, New York, NY 10012, by arrangement with G. P. Putnam's Sons, an imprint of
Penguin Young Readers Group, a division of Penguin Random House LLC. SCHOLASTIC and
associated logos are trademarks and/or registered trademarks of Scholastic Inc.

12 11 10 9 8 7 6 5 4 3   18 19 20 21 22

Printed in the U.S.A.   40

First Scholastic printing, September 2017

Design by Ryan Thomann
Text set in Markin
The art was done with Sumi brush work on rice paper and completed in Adobe Photoshop.

BEWARE

HENSEL AND GRETEL NINJA CHICKS

Corey Rosen Schwartz and Rebecca J. Gomez

illustrated by Dan Santat

SCHOLASTIC INC.

Once upon a menacing time

two chicks knew a fox was at large.
Their Ma had been taken
and Pop was quite shaken
so Hensel and Gretel took charge.

They trained in the art of **ninjutsu** and practiced their wing throws and blocks.

They learned how to creep
without making a peep
so they wouldn't fall prey to that fox.

One day they returned from the dojo
to a coop in complete disarray.
The signs of a tussle
showed someone with muscle
had dragged
their dear papa
away!

They quickly surveyed their surroundings.
The fox had left prints in the dirt!
"Come on, we're not chicken!
That fox needs a lickin'
before our poor papa gets hurt!"

They trekked till
they spotted a feather.

It looks like
we're on
the right track!

They kept up the chase,
dropping crumbs, just in case,
so they'd easily find their way back.

The forest grew twisted and tangled
as Hensel and Gretel searched on.
The light faded fast
and they noticed at last
that the trail—
and the breadcrumbs—
were GONE!

They shuddered and
groped in the darkness.
"We're lost!" whispered
Hensel with dread.

They weaved and they wound,
and kept roaming around
until they saw light up ahead.

"I'll whip up some quick teriyaki,
while we wait for the tea cakes to bake."
"Why not?" Hensel reckoned,
off-guard for a second.

Then quickly,
she saw her **mistake!**

She gasped, and then dashed
to the corner,
where Pop was confined in a crate.

"Watch out!" Papa cried.

"You'll be
chicken-pot-pied!"

She sidestepped,
but it was too late.

The fox plucked her up in a hurry
and shoved her right into the pen.

You're scrawny and tough,
but you'll plump soon enough.
For now, I'll just stir-fry this hen!

The fluttering hen looked familiar.
"It's Mama!"
cried Hensel
in shock.

Hensel was scared,
but she came well-prepared.

I bet I can
jimmy this lock.

Outside in the dark, Gretel listened,
dismayed at the fox's misdeed.
She climbed to the flue
and squeezed her way through

with **ninja-like silence** and **speed**.

Then Gretel swooped in
and snatched Mama
and swiftly adjusted her stance.

The fox took a **leap**,

"Not bad," said the fox, striding toward them.
"Give up!" Gretel clucked, undeterred.

The fox said, "Surrender?
No way, **chicken tender!**
Your cheep little threats are absurd!"

The fox charged and grappled with Gretel—
a flurry of feathers and fur.

The fox held her tight,
but Gretel wrenched right

as something zipped past with a whir!

With the fox in a daze, Gretel vaulted
as Hensel and Papa broke free.

She slammed the door shut
and then locked it.

The fox crumpled, looking unnerved.

"You two Ninja Chicks
got us out of that fix,
and **justice**—not dinner—was served."

From then on they made it their mission
to **rescue**, **protect** and defend.
They'd work night and day
to liberate prey
till bird-napping came to an end.